Farmer Brown

Written by Dave Closser
Illustrated by Brigit Galloy

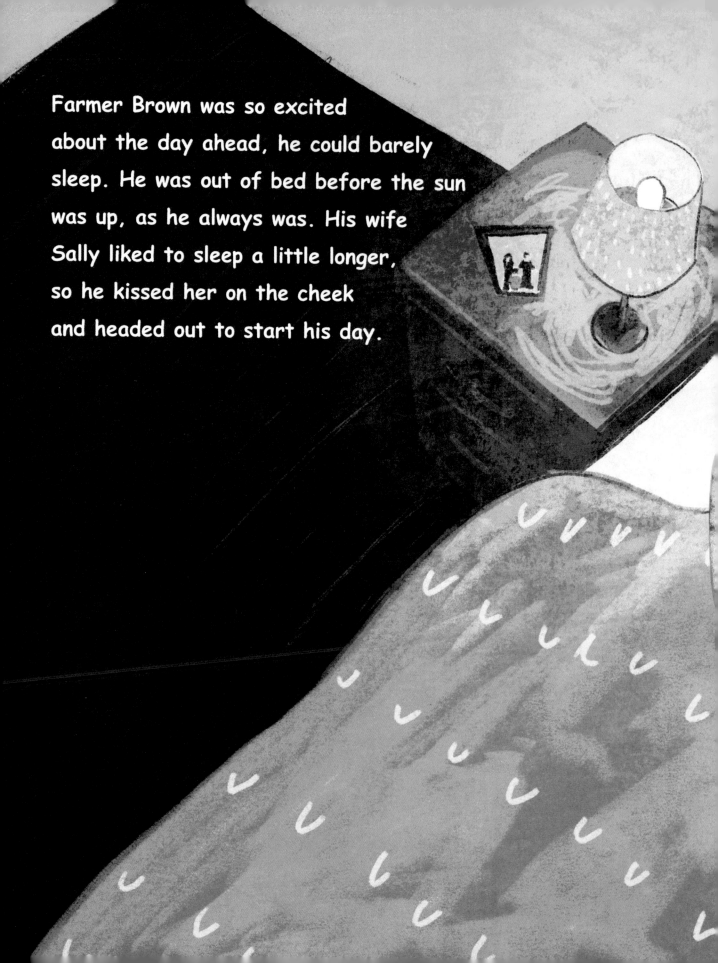

Farmer Brown was so excited about the day ahead, he could barely sleep. He was out of bed before the sun was up, as he always was. His wife Sally liked to sleep a little longer, so he kissed her on the cheek and headed out to start his day.

Farmer Brown had taken over
the farm his father had left to him. But
as hard as he tried, he had never been a very
good farmer. This year had been different. He had
worked extra hard and his corn stalks were taller than ever
before. And each stalk held many large ears of corn. He knew
his father would have been proud of him.

But before he started up his tractor to begin harvesting his beautiful corn crop, he had friends to tend to. When he opened the door to leave his house, 2 pigs, 3 sheep and 4 goats were waiting in the dark to greet him. He also had 20 chickens, but like Sally, they liked to sleep in until the sun was up.

With pigs, sheep and goats all playing together, they walked to the special barn he had built for his animal friends. Farmer Brown mixed up the special blend of food he made fresh every day. The pigs, sheep and goats waiting patiently by their bowls as he filled each one.

After feeding his pigs, sheep and goats, Farmer Brown headed across the barnyard to feed his chickens. As much as he loved all his animals, his chickens may have been his favorites. Most farmers have chickens so they can lay eggs, to sell to make money. Not Farmer Brown. He had chickens because he liked his chickens. He never expected them to lay eggs.

Most farmers also make their chickens live crammed together in small chicken coops where they have no freedom to move about. Not Farmer Brown. He had built his chickens a small house that even had a hot tub on the roof, just for his chickens! His chickens loved their house.

Of course, the chickens also had their own very special food mixture, also made fresh every day. Farmer Brown would mix the best grains then add apples and strawberries cut up into very small pieces. Finally, he would add just a little honey to make it sweeter, and healthier. Each chicken had a bowl with their name on it next to their bed. Farmer Brown filled their bowls so their breakfast would be waiting when they woke up.

The sun was starting to rise now and it was time. He was going to harvest the best corn crop he'd ever grown! He headed across the barnyard to an old barn where he kept his tractor. As he walked, he thought this may be the year he would actually be able to make enough money selling his corn to replace his old tired tractor. His tractor still worked, but it was slow and would sometimes get stuck in the mud.

He climbed up on his old friend, turned the key and it started right up. He backed out of the barn and headed to his nearby corn field. But as he drove, he felt a few drops of rain. By the time he reached his field it was raining hard. He knew he'd have to wait until the rain stopped to begin his harvest, so he drove his tractor back to the barn. Farmer Brown was a patient man. He could wait until the rain stopped.

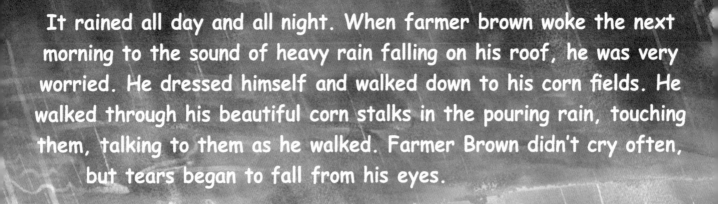

It rained all day and all night. When farmer brown woke the next morning to the sound of heavy rain falling on his roof, he was very worried. He dressed himself and walked down to his corn fields. He walked through his beautiful corn stalks in the pouring rain, touching them, talking to them as he walked. Farmer Brown didn't cry often, but tears began to fall from his eyes.

He had worked so hard this year and had been so proud of the corn he'd grown. But he now knew his corn would go bad before he could get his old tractor in the field to harvest it. His feet were even getting stuck in the deep mud, so his tractor would surely get stuck.

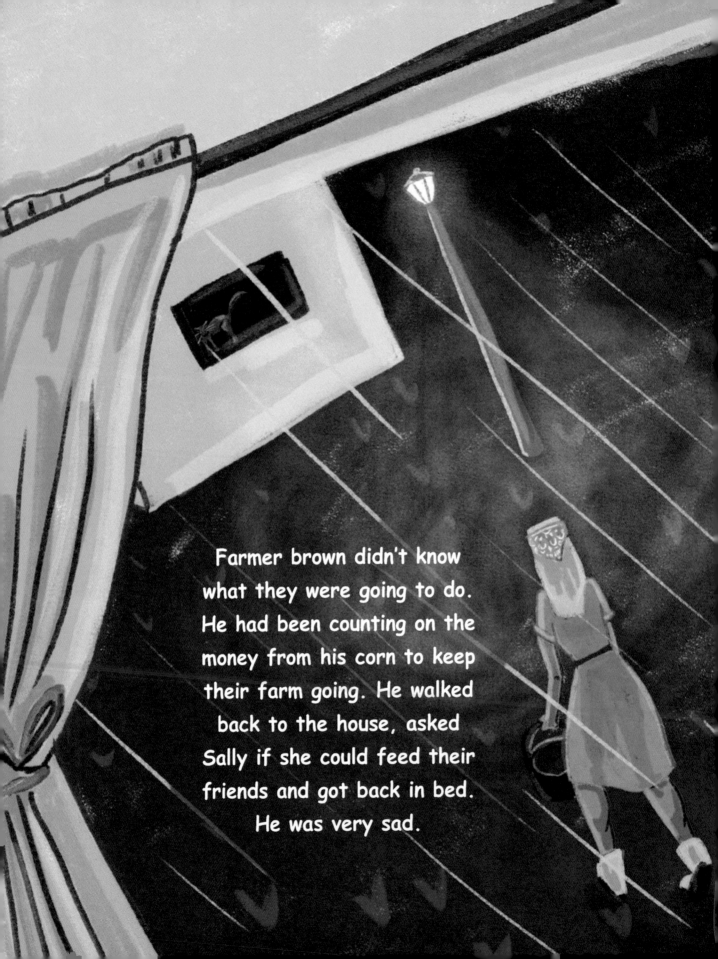

Farmer brown didn't know
what they were going to do.
He had been counting on the
money from his corn to keep
their farm going. He walked
back to the house, asked
Sally if she could feed their
friends and got back in bed.
He was very sad.

Sally headed out in the pouring rain and fed the pigs, sheep and goats first. Then she went to feed the chickens. She had never fed them before, but she made the fresh food just like Farmer Brown did. They liked Sally, but no one other than Farmer Brown had ever fed them. The chickens knew something was terribly wrong. After eating, they all decided to meet in the hot tub on the roof, in the rain.

They didn't know what was wrong, but they wanted to do something to help. They had never laid eggs, but somehow they knew this was something they were probably supposed to do. Maybe this could help. So together they decided they would stay in their nests and lay eggs.

The next day when Sally fed the chickens she was surprised to find 2 eggs under every chicken. They were shiny, a golden color, and almost sparkly. Sally had never seen such beautiful eggs. She collected all 40 eggs and took them down to the local market to see if she could sell them. But they looked so different than normal eggs she didn't know if the market would have any interest. The woman at the market thought they were beautiful too and said she'd try.

The next day Sally found 4 eggs under each chicken. She gathered up all 80 eggs and took them to the market, not knowing if the eggs she left the day before had even been sold. When she arrived at the market there was a line of people waiting to get in. The lady that owned the market said all these people had been waiting for Sally's eggs. Apparently word had spread fast that Sally's eggs were the most beautiful and the best tasting around!

The rain finally stopped, and Farmer Brown felt good enough to feed his animal friends again. The first morning he walked out his door into the darkness, his pigs, sheep and goats were running in circles around him. They were so excited to see him again! He fed the pigs, sheep and goats then headed to the chicken house. As soon as he walked in the door, the chickens knew right away it was Farmer Brown. They all got up together and flapped their wings in delight. They too were so happy to see him again! Today he found 6 eggs under each chicken. He just didn't know what had gotten into his little feathered friends. He collected all 120 eggs and took them to the market himself.

After a few more weeks the chickens finally stopped laying eggs. Farmer Brown and Sally had just been throwing the money they made from selling the eggs in a big box under the kitchen table. They decided to sit down and count the money. Together it took them hours. When they were finally done, they realized the money they made selling eggs was the same amount they would have made had they been able to sell their beautiful corn crop. They both looked at each other, smiled at first, then burst out laughing! There was enough to buy food for themselves and their animals, with enough left over for a new tractor!

A few weeks
later as Farmer
Brown was backing
his brand-new tractor
into the barn he thought
of his father. He wondered
if his dad would have been
disappointed with
his son.

He had spent years teaching Farmer Brown how to be a good
farmer. But Farmer Brown still hadn't harvested a good corn crop
like his father did almost every year. Not paying attention, Farmer
Brown bumped his tractor into something in the back of the barn.
He turned the engine off and jumped down to see what he hit. He
had knocked over a few of the signs his father used to hang on the
barn back when Farmer Brown was a child. The signs hadn't made a
lot of sense to him when he was young. He had completely forgotten
they were still stacked in the barn.

If you live your life treating all with love, kindness and respect, you will have lived a good life

As he read the words on the sign that had fallen over he smiled. Happy tears started to run down his cheeks. He missed his dad.

About the Author

Dave was educated in engineering and used his degree in the computer business for several years. But much of his working career has been spent in the building industry. At present he spends his days in his shop designing and building custom cabinets and furniture. He also spends a great deal of time outdoors pursuing his passion for photography. Farmer Brown is the first childrens book, or book of any kind he has published.

Dedication

To my son Daniel who as a toddler awakened my imagination with his insatiable desire for "Made Up" bedtime stories. Farmer Brown is just one of many I shared with him in my attempt to get him to sleep...

The author with his son on a mountain top approximately
25 years after this story was first told

Made in the USA
Coppell, TX
20 October 2021